Way Out West with Pirate Pete and Pirate Joe

A Viking Easy-to-Read

by A. E. Cannon

illustrated by Elwood H. Smith

VIKING

To my son Dylan
—A.E.C.

To my dad, a B-Western hero
—E.H.S.

VIKING
Published by Penguin Group
Penguin Young Readers Group, 345 Hudson Street, New York, New York 10014, U.S.A.
Penguin Group (Canada), 90 Eglinton Avenue East, Toronto, Ontario, Canada M4P 2Y3
(a division of Pearson Penguin Canada Inc.)
Penguin Books Ltd, 80 Strand, London WC2R 0RL, England
Penguin Ireland, 25 St Stephen's Green, Dublin 2, Ireland
(a division of Penguin Books Ltd)
Penguin Group (Australia), 250 Camberwell Road, Camberwell,
Victoria 3124, Australia (a division of Pearson Australia Group Pty Ltd)
Penguin Books India Pvt Ltd, 11 Community Centre, Panchsheel Park,
New Delhi – 110 017, India
Penguin Group (NZ), Cnr Airborne and Rosedale Roads, Albany,
Auckland 1310, New Zealand (a division of Pearson New Zealand Ltd)
Penguin Books (South Africa) (Pty) Ltd, 24 Sturdee Avenue, Rosebank,
Johannesburg 2196, South Africa

First published in 2006 by Viking, a division of Penguin Young Readers Group

1 3 5 7 9 10 8 6 4 2

LIBRARY OF CONGRESS CATALOGING-IN-PUBLICATION DATA
Cannon, A. E. (Ann Edwards).
Way out West with Pirate Pete and Pirate Joe / by A.E. Cannon ;
illustrated by Elwood H. Smith.
p.   cm.
Summary: Two silly pirates go on a search for their Wild
West cousins and end up at a surprise birthday party.
ISBN 0-670-06080-1 (hardcover)
[1. Pirates—Fiction. 2. Birthdays—Fiction. 3. West (U.S.)—Fiction.
4. Humorous stories.] I. Smith, Elwood H., date– ill. II. Title.
PZ7.C17135Way 2006
[E]—dc22
2005018085

Manufactured in China
Set in Bookman

Pirate Pete and Pirate Joe live in a city

by the sea with their pirate pets—

Studley, Dudley, and Bucko.

Every day Pirate Pete and Pirate Joe

do their pirate chores.

When they are done, Pirate Pete

and Pirate Joe visit their mother,

the Pirate Queen.

The Pirate Queen cooks crabs and eels

for Pirate Pete and Pirate Joe.

For herself she makes jellyfish on toast.

After lunch everyone dances and sings
songs of the sea.

By the time Pirate Pete and Pirate Joe
leave, they are happy!

Except for today.

When he gets home, Pirate Joe checks
the mailbox.

"Boo-hoo!" says Pirate Joe.

"Why are you so blue?" asks
Mailman Brad.

"Today is my birthday!" says Pirate Joe.

"Silly pirate," says Mailman Brad. "You should be glad!"

"But everyone forgot!" says Pirate Joe.

"Oh, no!" says Mailman Brad.

He digs deep into his mailman bag.

"Is there a birthday card for me?" asks Pirate Joe.

"Too bad. So sad," says Mailman Brad. "No cards for you."

"Boo-hoo!" says Pirate Joe.

"Wait!" says Mailman Brad. "Here's a letter."

Mailman Brad gives Pirate Joe the letter and waves good-bye.

He does not say "Happy birthday."

"Even Mailman Brad forgot," says Pirate Joe. He hangs his head and goes inside.

"What does the letter say?" asks

Pirate Pete.

Pirate Joe opens it and reads.

WANTED:

PIRATE PETE AND PIRATE JOE, TO FIND
COWBOY CLETE AND COWBOY MOE!

Cowboy Clete and Cowboy Moe are the

pirates' cousins.

Cowboy Clete likes to line dance.

Cowboy Moe loves to clog.

"Are the cowboys lost?" asks

Pirate Pete.

Pirate Joe reads the rest.

Dear Pirates,

The cowboys are missing!
They were last seen leaving
school (early) with
Tumbleweed Ted and his
gang of Rude Dudes!
Please help us find them!

From,
The Rodeo Queen (their ma)
Cowpoke Carl (their pa)

"Oh, no!" says Pirate Pete.

"AAAAARGH!" says Pirate Joe.

He does not care that the Rodeo Queen
and Cowpoke Carl forgot his birthday.
He wants to find Tumbleweed Ted.
Tumbleweed Ted is bad!
"We are mean!" says Pirate Joe.
"We are not clean!" says Pirate Pete.
"We are not sweet!" says Pirate Joe.
"We have stinky feet!" says Pirate Pete.
The pirates rattle their swords.

The pirates call for their pets.

"Now, Dasher! Now, Dancer! Now,

Prancer and Vixen!" says Pirate Joe.

"Wrong pets!" says Pirate Pete.

The pirates call for the right pets.

The pirates and the right pirate pets

jump into their black van, the Jolly Roger.

These pirates are ready for action!

"Go west, young man!" says Pirate Pete.

"Who cares about my birthday anyway?!"

says Pirate Joe.

"Yo ho!" says Bucko.

And away they go.

Pirate Pete and Pirate Joe go west.

"Westward ho!" says Pirate Joe.

They drive to the cowboy cousins'

home. It is called Rattlesnake Ranch.

Cowpoke Carl, the Rodeo Queen, and

their pet bull, Hoppy, greet the pirates.

"YEE-HAW!" hollers the Rodeo Queen.

"Yoo-hoo, little lady," say Pirate Pete
and Pirate Joe.

"Yippee," whistles Cowpoke Carl.

Cowpoke Carl has no teeth.

"Yahoo, partner!" say Pirate Pete and
Pirate Joe.

"Snort, snort," says Hoppy.

The Rodeo Queen feeds Hoppy a carrot.

"I did not know that big bulls ate carrots," says Pirate Pete.

"THIS BIG BULL THINKS HE'S A BIG RABBIT!" hollers the Rodeo Queen.

Hoppy hops.

Hop. Hop. Hop.

Pirate Pete pets Hoppy.

"Nice bunny," says Pirate Joe.

"Tell us about Tumbleweed Ted," says Pirate Pete.

"Tumbleweed Ted and his gang are rude dudes," whistles Cowpoke Carl.

"THEY LIVE AT THE RUDE DUDES' DUDE RANCH!" hollers the Rodeo Queen.

"What do rude dudes do at the Rude Dudes' Dude Ranch?" says Pirate Pete.

"THEY BURP AND THEY SLURP!" hollers the Rodeo Queen.

"Aaaaargh!" say the pirates.

"They snore and they bore!" whistles Cowpoke Carl.

"Bigger aaaaargh!" say the pirates.

"THEY MAKE A MESS BUT DON'T

CONFESS!" hollers the Rodeo Queen.

"Biggest aaaaargh!" say the pirates.

"We fear our boys will turn into rude

dudes, too," whistles Cowpoke Carl.

Pirate Pete and Pirate Joe rattle

their swords.

"No way!" says Pirate Pete.

"Pirate Birthday Boy will save the day!"

says Pirate Joe.

No one says "Happy birthday."

"We are mean!" says Pirate Pete.

"We are not clean!" says Pirate Joe.

"We are not sweet!" says Pirate Pete.

"We have stinky feet!" says Pirate Joe.

"Even on my birthday!"

Pirate Pete does the hornpipe.

Pirate Joe does the limbo.

Cowpoke Carl and the Rodeo Queen

do a square dance.

The pets all do the Bunny Hop.

"We want that Ted, alive or dead!" the
pirates shout.

The Rodeo Queen gives the pirates a
map of the Rude Dudes' Dude Ranch.
X marks the spot.

The pirates and their pets hop into
the Jolly Roger. Hoppy hops in, too.

"Yo ho!" say Pirate Pete and Pirate Joe.

"YEE-HAW!" hollers the Rodeo Queen.

"Yippee!" whistles Cowpoke Carl. "Get
along, little doggies!"

Pirate Joe turns the map upside down.

"Go this way," he says.

Pirate Joe turns the map right-side up.

"Go that way," he says.

The pirates drive for miles and miles.

They see cows.

"Moo," say the cows.

"How now, brown cows," says Pirate Joe.

"Snort, snort," says Hoppy.

They see ponies.

"Can I have a pony for my birthday?"
says Pirate Joe.

"Hint, hint," says Bucko.

Pirate Pete and Pirate Joe see signs.

"Sticks and stones may break my
bones!" says Pirate Pete. "But signs
will never hurt me!"

"What he said!" says Pirate Joe.

The pirates see a mountain. It is called

Old Smokey. On top of Old Smokey

sits the Rude Dudes' Dude Ranch.

The pirates park in front of the Rude

Dudes' Dude Ranch.

They get out and ring the doorbell.

"Ding-dong! Pirates calling!" says

Pirate Pete.

No one answers.

Pirate Pete pushes the door open.

Creak. Creak. Creak.

The pirates creep inside.

Creep. Creep. Creep.

It is dark. The pirates cannot see.

Suddenly there is a noise.

"Did you make that sound?" asks
Pirate Joe.

"No!" says Pirate Pete.

"Then who did?" asks Pirate Joe.

The lights go on.

The room is filled with balloons!

Presents! People!

"SURPRISE!" the people shout.

Pirate Joe leaps into Pirate Pete's arms.

"Eek! Squeak! Shriek!" says Pirate Joe.

"HAPPY BIRTHDAY, PIRATE JOE!" the
people shout, and clap their hands.

"This here's a party for Pirate Joe,"
says Cowboy Clete.

"This here's a party because we love
him so," says Cowboy Moe.

"HAPPY BIRTHDAY, BIRTHDAY BOY!"
booms the Pirate Queen.

"Here's a birthday joke for you," says the Rodeo Queen. "What do you get when you put four quarter horses together?"

"A one-dollar-bill horse!" says Pirate Joe.

"Good math!" whistles Cowpoke Carl. Cowboy Clete and Cowboy Moe and Pirate Pete hand Pirate Joe a present. Cowboy boots!

"These boots are made for walking!" says Pirate Joe.

"WRONG!" hollers the Rodeo Queen.
"THOSE BOOTS ARE MADE FOR
DANCING!"
The Quicksand Band strikes up a song.
Everyone dances by the light of the
surprise-party moon!